MR. NOISY
and the Silent Night

originated by Roger Hargreaves

W9-AML-972

Written and illustrated by Adam Hargreaves

PSS!

PRICE STERN SLOAN

An Imprint of Penguin Random House

Mr. Quiet is a sensitive fellow.

Loud noises make him very nervous.

Unfortunately for Mr. Quiet, he lives in a place called Loudland.

Which is exactly that.

LOUD!

And at Christmastime, Loudland is an especially loud place.

Which means that Mr. Quiet, unlike you and me, does not look forward to Christmas.

Poor Mr. Quiet.

At Christmastime there are all the Christmas card deliveries, delivered by the Loudland mailman, Mr. Stamp.

He is not called Mr. Stamp because of the stamps you put on envelopes, but because he stamps his feet as he delivers the mail.

STAMP! STAMP! STAMP! up Mr. Quiet's path.

SLAM! would go the mailbox.

And then STAMP! STAMP! STAMP! back down the path.

Every morning.

For weeks!

There were all the jolly Loudland people greeting one another on the street.

"MERRY CHRISTMAS!"

"MERRY CHRISTMAS TO YOU!"

"AND A HAPPY NEW YEAR!"

They were so loud that it was like being at a football game.

And there were the carolers.

In Loudland, the carolers do not just sing.

They bellow!

At the very top of their voices.

Poor Mr. Quiet would turn out the lights and hide behind his couch and pretend he was not at home.

But he could still hear them.

And to make matters even worse, every year,
Mr. Noisy would come to stay.

Mr. Noisy lives in a place where they do not like
noise. He likes to go to Loudland for his Christmas
vacation where he can be as loud as he likes.
Which, as you can imagine, is very loud indeed!

On Christmas morning, Mr. Noisy would turn on the radio at full volume and sing along to the Christmas carols.

It was so loud, it made the teacups rattle in their saucers!

You could have heard Mr. Noisy in another country!

Then there was Christmas lunch.

And Christmas firecrackers!

Loudland Christmas firecrackers.

BANG!

BANG!

They sounded like cannons being fired.

And of course, Mr. Noisy eats with his mouth open.

CHOMP! CHOMP! CHOMP! through the turkey.

CHOMP! CHOMP! CHOMP! through the Christmas pudding.

What a racket.

Mr. Noisy could not even open his presents quietly.

CRACKLE! CRACKLE! CRACKLE! went the paper each time he unwrapped one.

Poor Mr. Quiet.

But that was last Christmas.

This Christmas, something different happened.

Something magical.

It snowed!

Now, everyone likes snow, but this year it snowed and snowed and snowed until all the roads were deep with snow, right to the top of the bushes.

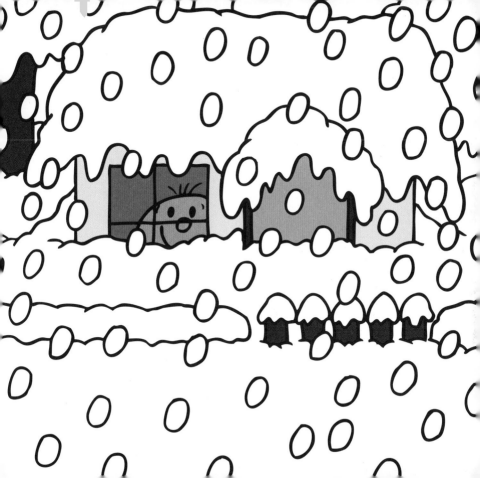

Which caused chaos.

But not for Mr. Quiet.

Things went really well for Mr. Quiet.

There was no loud Mr. Stamp.

He was stuck at the post office.

There were no loud jolly people in the streets.

They were all stuck at home.

And there were no loud carolers.

They got stuck in the snow.

But the very best thing of all was a phone call from Mr. Noisy saying that he wouldn't be able to come to visit.

So this year, Mr. Quiet had a very quiet Christmas.

No loud radio.

No loud Christmas firecrackers.

No loud chomping at dinner.

And no loud, crackling wrapping paper.

The only thing that Mr. Quiet could hear, very faintly, was the sound of caroling.

Very quiet caroling.

Just the sort of caroling that Mr. Quiet likes.

Who was it?

Why, it was Mr. Noisy.

I told you, you could hear him from another country!

And what was Mr. Noisy singing?

Take a guess . . .

That's right!

"Silent Night"!